DERRYDALE BOOKS
New York/Avenel, New Jersey
Copyright © 1992 by Peter Haddock Ltd, England
All rights reserved.
This 1992 edition is published by Derrydale Books.
distributed by Outlet Book Company, Inc.,
a Random House Company,
40 Engelhard Avenue
Avenel, New Jersey 07001.

Printed and Bound in Singapore

ISBN: 0-517-08665-4

8 7 6 5 4 3 2 1

Beauty & The Beast

Retold & Illustrated by John Patience

Once there was a rich merchant who had three daughters. Two were proud and lazy. The third and youngest was kind, considerate and hardworking.

Now it happened that the merchant lost all his money and the family was forced to move into a poky little cottage. The two eldest sisters did nothing but complain, but the youngest – who was called Beauty – looked after them all and comforted her poor father who was troubled by bills which he could not pay.

One day the merchant was offered work in a distant town. Filled with excitement he prepared for his journey. "Bring us back some fine dresses, hats and shoes!" cried the eldest sisters. "And what would you like, Beauty?" asked her father. "Come back safely and bring me a red rose," replied Beauty.

But the merchant's good luck did not last. It was mid-winter and, as he was passing through a deep forest, the snow began to fall. In the gloom he strayed from the pathway and became lost! Just as the merchant was giving up hope of ever seeing his family again, he saw through the swirling snow the lights of a great castle. He rode to the door and called out, but there was no answer. He stabled his horse and entered the castle. "Hello! Is anyone here?" he called, but he heard only the echo of his own voice. He found a table laid with food. He was very hungry so he ate but, though he saw no-one, he had the feeling that he was being watched. At last, tired out from his journey, he slept.

When the merchant woke the next morning he found a costume of fine clothes laid out for him. He ate a good breakfast and then went to the stable to find his horse. On his way he passed through the gardens. Though it was the middle of winter the flowers were all in bloom and not a leaf had fallen. Remembering his promise to Beauty, he stopped to pick a rose. At once there was a terrible noise. He turned and saw a monstrous beast. "Have I not given you enough, that you must steal the flowers from my garden?" roared the Beast. "I have a mind to kill you right now!" The merchant fell down on his knees and begged for mercy. "Your life will be spared," said the Beast, "if one of your daughters will offer to live with me here. Go now and let them choose. Do not try to cheat me or I will hunt you down and kill you!"

The merchant returned to his family with a heavy heart. He told them his story of the castle and the terrible Beast. Beauty could not bear to see her father so downcast. "Don't worry," she said softly. "I will go to live with the Beast. I am sure no harm will come to me." Naturally her father protested but Beauty insisted.

The following day the merchant and his daughter returned to the strange castle. The Beast was pleased. He gave Beauty fine dresses to wear and to the merchant he gave a chest of gold but he told him he must leave the castle and never return. Sadly, Beauty kissed her father goodbye.

So began Beauty's life in the castle. And as the days passed she grew fond of the Beast. Though he was frightening to look at, he was kind and gentle. In the evenings the Beast would play beautiful music and tell her stories of the strange lands through which he had travelled, while she sat by the fire and worked at her embroidery.

Still Beauty wished that one day a handsome young prince would come along to rescue her. Then one night she had a strange dream. An old woman appeared to her and said, "Do not judge by appearances. What is ugly on the outside may be beautiful inside." In the morning Beauty thought about the dream, but mistakenly she decided it was not important.

One misty morning the Beast found Beauty crying in the garden. "What is the matter?" he asked. "Your roses are beautiful," she replied, "but they remind me that if I had not asked my father to bring me back a rose I would not be your prisoner here." "Must you think of yourself as a prisoner? Don't you know that I love you? Will you marry me?" asked the Beast. "No, I cannot marry you," said Beauty. "You are so ugly." Then the Beast bowed his great head and wandered sadly away.

The next day Beauty found a mirror. She looked into it and there she saw her father lying ill. That evening she told the Beast what she had seen and begged to be allowed to visit her father. The Beast reluctantly agreed, providing that Beauty promised to return. So it was that the following morning Beauty left the castle. "Remember your poor Beast who loves you," cried the Beast, "and return within three weeks."

When Beauty arrived home her father was indeed very ill. However, as soon as she was there to care for him he quickly began to recover. The weeks passed by and Beauty forgot her promise to the Beast. Then one night she had a dream. She saw the Beast lying dying under a tree in the castle gardens and all around him the leaves were falling and the sky was as heavy as lead. Beauty awoke horrified! She rushed to her horse and rode like the wind to the castle. There she found the Beast lying dying, just as in her dream.

"Dear Beast," cried Beauty, "I did not realise before that I love you. Now I fear I have killed you." Beauty's tears fell upon the Beast's rough fur and slowly he began to revive. "Beauty, have you come back to me? Will you marry me now?" he whispered. "Yes, dear Beast," she replied.

Then there was a blaze of light, the Beast disappeared and in his place was a handsome prince. "I was bewitched," explained the prince, "by a spell that could only be broken when someone loved me in spite of my ugliness!"

Soon afterwards the prince and Beauty were married. Her father and her sisters came to the celebrations and they all lived happily ever after.